Clint Faraday Mysteries
book 6
Storm Front

There is a storm front approaching from the southeast. A boatload of cocaine is forced in to near Bocas. There is a torture-murder. Everyone except Clint believes that the two things are connected. At first.

Contents

Dawn — pg. 1
Doesn't Compute — pg. 4
The Second Body — pg. 18
Isla Popa et al — pg. 33
Maps to Nowhere — pg. 45
Glittering Morsels — pg. 63
Back to the Grind — pg. 69

About the author

CD Moulton has traveled extensively over much of the world both in the music business, where he was a rock guitarist, songwriter and arranger and in an import/export business. He has been everything from a bar owner to auto salvage (junkyard) manager, longshoreman to high steel worker, orchid grower to landscaper, tropical fish farmer to commercial fisherman. He started writing books in 1983 and has published more than 350 books as of January 1, 2023. His most popular books to date are about research with orchids, though much of his science fiction and fantasy work has proven popular. He wrote the CD Grimes, PI series, and the Det. Nick Storie series, Clint Faraday series, and many other works.

He now resides in Gualaca, Chiriqui, Panamá, where he writes books, plays music with friends, does research with orchids and medicinal plants. He has lately become involved in fighting for the rights of the indigenous people, who are among his closest friends, and in fighting the extreme corruption in the courts and police in Panamá.

He offers the free e-book, *Fading Paradise*, that explains what he has been through because of the corruption.

CD is the discoverer of the Chadam Protocol for curing cancer.

Facebook page Ambrosia peruviana for cancer.

Storm Front

Dawn

"Clint, did you have the TV on?" Judi Lum, Clint's neighbor in Bocas del Toro, called from her deck on Saigon Bay to Clint Faraday, retired PI from Florida, who was on his own deck. He called back that he didn't turn the thing on unless he expected something special.

"On the news. There's a storm front coming in from the southeast. It seems to be a pretty bad one. They're trying to call all the boats in to port. Nasty."

"Bad enough for us to worry about?" he asked. She didn't know. She would watch it.

Clint finished his coffee and hojaldres and flipped on the radio to the emergency channel to be sure there was no call that he should respond to. There was a lot of chatter, but of very short duration. People were calling to say they were alright, then would leave the channel clear for emergency and m'aidez calls. He heard the police break that said for all officers to monitor channel ess2. That meant that it came from the US Coast guard, so someone was in trouble, or there was some illegal activity they observed. They would call for the Panamanian police to respond, in those cases.

This was that a fast cigarette boat was headed in at the Zapatillas. It was suspected of being a drug carrier. One passenger. Male. Had automatic weapon(s). Fifteen minutes later, the police chopper, coming back from searching to warn boaters, radioed that the boat was between Bastimentos and Solarte and had run up on a piece of reef. The police boats were dispatched and ordered to take no chances. If they were fired on, they were to return fire and were to shoot to kill, in all instances.

Ten minutes later, a boat reported that the boat had no one aboard. There were large packages, wrapped in plastic. There were four synchronized two hundred fifty horsepower outboards that had been running it. The bottom was holed, but would not sink further, as the coral head would hold it where it was. There was a plastic cover for an inflatable on board, so the passenger had, apparently, gone ashore somewhere in it. The other boats were to fan out and search the shoreline on both of the islands. No such craft had come anywhere close to either end of the bay between the islands, so it was there.

Almost an hour later, as the wind was kicking up very strongly, they found the inflatable near the shore of Solarte, under the mangroves. No one was in it. It was being processed. The passenger could not go far, there. It was as much as impenetrable. There was no evidence of a path being chopped onto the island, at the shoreline, but the passenger could have made his way inland past the mangroves that fringed the island and could move a good distance. He was trapped. They would find him.

Fifteen minutes later, a body was discovered a short distance from the inflatable. The man had been shot in the head. There was no identification on him. There were signs he had been tortured before being shot.

That seemed strange, to Clint. There wouldn't have been time to torture anyone. There was only one passenger on that boat, meaning the body would have to be the pilot or someone who chanced on him – which made torture ridiculous.

He had to finish battening down his stuff. He didn't think much about it.

Then.

The storm was coming onshore strongly, now. Clint rode his Ducatti to the police station to be there if they needed help. People could act like idiots, with a storm coming. Already, Sergio had arrested four surfers who were headed out for a thrill ride. The raging surf would grind them to hamburger on the reefs. Idiots!

Sergio told Clint what they knew. It wasn't a lot, and it was. It depends on which angle you chose to view it. Clint could see Sergio's point, that there was little reason to investigate a drug killing. You either caught them in the act or there would be no prosecution of the case, due to lack of evidence. It wasted the time and resources of the police department.

Clint said he agreed one hundred percent, but there was no evidence this killing had anything to do with drugs and druggies.

Sergio said they had scoured the parts of Solarte, where the runner could have gone. He wasn't there. The body was probably the runner. He was supposed to meet someone, there. The someone didn't care to take the chance of being identified and took care of that problem.

Clint said that left the torture bit. There was definitely no time for anyone to torture anyone. Sergio shrugged. He said Clint could look into it, if he wanted. Clint had little else to do, so he would look into it.

The calls started coming in about the storm damage. Nothing too serious. Clint waited it out at the station, with the police. He knew most of them. When it was fairly certain the storm would stay under anything that could cause particularly bad effects on the island, Clint went home. It was just after three AM, so he slept until almost nine. Extremely late for him. The main part of the storm had passed. It was a drizzly morning, with little patches of sunlight, here and there.

His battery went dead on his boat sometime during the night. The pump stopped. There were almost two feet of water in it he had to bail.

He put the battery on the charger. It was totally discharged from being under water. He used the hand pump to finish bailing. The rain wouldn't completely stop for the day. There would be small heavy rains for a couple of minutes, then it would drop back to the way it was, at present. He would have it to do again until he had the battery charged. He thought about it, and went into town to buy another battery. It would be smart to have a backup. He usually thought of that kind of thing before it was needed.

He stopped at the station, but there was nothing new. The autopsy wouldn't be done until the next day. The lab had suffered a bit of water damage. It had to be repaired before much of it could be used.

Clint went to the Golden Grill to listen to the local gossip. There wasn't much. Everybody was talking about the storm and how it wasn't anything to the one back in etc. etc. etc. There was a little talk about the drug boat. More than half a ton of fully processed cocaine. Worth more than fifteen million, even before it was cut, like it would have been. Clint figured it at the going wholesale price. About eight hundred thousand. Two million on the streets. There was some talk about someone trying to get some land on Isla Popa by killing off some people, brought out because of Wild Bill having done that. Somebody was missing. That kind of thing was still around, but less than there was a few years ago. They talked a little about the body and what was going to happen to all that dope.

He asked if they had any idea who the body might have been. Jim said he was sure it wasn't the runner, like the cops said. They just didn't want to be bothered. The runner was alone on the boat, so who would have killed him?

"Maybe a rival drug dealer," Thom suggested. Jim said that made even less sense.

Clint left before the argument started. He went to The Pirate and chatted with a few people. Same general ideas. No one knew of anyone who had gone missing from Solarte. It was noticed very quickly when anyone was missing, now that Wild Bill's exploits and murders were known.

There was nothing more to be done, now, so he went home to relax a bit and call all the people he knew the storm might have affected. It appeared the front was a series of waves that would come in about one every ten hours for two more, so it wouldn't be very smart to relax. The up side was that it wasn't one broad band, like the innundation two years past. There would be damage to the roads and things on the river banks, but not extensive, like before.

Clint then went to the morgue to talk with Dr. Avanzas, who was presently doing the autopsies. He said the body's time of death couldn't be established within more than six hours, because of the sudden cooling from the storm. It was so long before the body was brought in that lividity couldn't determine much. The torture was with cuts and crushing the finger bones and burns, accomplished over a period of at least an hour.

Probably closer to two hours. That ruled out the drug boat having anything to do with it. Clint went to the station and reported on the information from Doc. He said that meant the runner had someone there to pick him up. He left the inflatable to make them concentrate on searching Solarte for a bit of time to allow him to escape. If the person who picked him up had tried to exit the alley by either end, he would have been seen. It was someone on either Solarte or Bastimentos. No one had any idea who it might have been.

The wind was picking up strongly as Clint headed back home. The next band was coming in.

Clint called a friend, who was a secret agent for Interpol, so knew much of what was going on in the area, particularly concerning drugs. He said the shipment was probably from the Peruvian connection going out of Medillin. He didn't have much information, except that a large shipment was supposed to go or have gone. Clint thanked him and decided to forget it until the fronts were past. He had a lot to occupy him, simply keeping his stuff secure. This was supposed to be a little worse than the first. The next one was back to about what the first was, if it didn't increase in the time it would take to reach Panamá.

The night was a bit noisier than the previous

night, but there was no more damage, of a major proportion. Clint checked with Judi and Ben, two neighbors who were also close friends. They didn't have any damage to report. Bocas could take a hell of a lot of wind and rain. Only the tourists worried much about it. He called Manny, a friend (who was an ex-mafia don who moved to Bocas to escape his past and raise a family who wouldn't be ashamed of how Pops made his) on Isla San Cristóbal, but he didn't have any damage to report, either, though he had spent most of the last two nights at the Indio village, helping to move the ones living in the lower parts onto higher ground. Miguel had come from Panamá City and had opened a building on his property for them and had slaughtered a pig, so they would have plenty of food. Manny took over a hundred pounds of rice. They grew onions, peppers, and such, right there. There were tons of yuca. Bananas and cocoa, yampi – it was all right there. Things were suave and tranquilo, at the moment.

That would let Clint concentrate on the body and what happened to him.

Clint went to Bastimentos in his boat, to check on friends there. Damage was a bit more severe. Bastimentos didn't have the natural protection Isla Colón had. It wasn't terrible. Clint was able to get a little information by asking something in passing and waiting for an opportunity to get the next question inserted. The recent capture of Wild Bill made that a good bit easier. He could ask who seemed strange in that way and who had been closer to Wild Bill. Not many on the island knew him. They wouldn't. Most are blacks, who he didn't seem to get along with, at all. The strangest ones associated with druggies and such were Quiroz and Larienze, two who were too often around the wrong people and the wrong places at the wrong times. Quite a number of the people there were minor street dealers, so knew something about people who moved there from Colón (The province, not Isla Colón) and who acted too much like assholes, all the time. Those two were living right in the middle of the area where so many were using and dealing in drugs, probably met with known biggies in the trade from time to time, yet claimed to not want anything to do with the locals of the same, if less elevated, type. In short, they were NOT liked, even a little bit.

Next was Solarte, where much the same was going on. He learned that there was one person who had a house out along the island a bit more than halfway, with his land going from the bay to the alley. He had docks on both sides. Strange things seemed to be going on at night on those docks. His name was McDonald. He was a Bahamian with a Jamaican wife.

Clint figured he had three viable candidates for suspects.

The next wave was coming in. Clint went back to Bocas Town, as the winds were getting strong. He secured the boat, went inside, took care of the e-mails and messages, then went to Judi's for dinner. Ben was there, as was Dave, their nutty musician friend. They talked about general things. Clint didn't bring up his case. It might be a good idea to keep his friends out of this one, though they could be a great help, in some cases. He didn't like that torture bit. If it weren't for that, they would already know all about it.

He went home, after the storm began to subside a little. Dave and Ben went to Ben's. Dave would go on home later, or would stay with Ben. Ben said, "Oh! Thrill!"

Ben's gay, in his mid twenties. Dave is in his seventies and had a girlfriend from back in Florida staying with him until she found a place in David or Boquete. They were all close and could share jokes and jibes that wouldn't offend. Clint grinned when he thought of how different it was in Florida, how phony the life and taboos there seemed here. There, if a man were to spend a night with a gay friend, he would be considered as being gay among most people. Here, nobody cared and nobody figured it was any of their business. The Indio saying was something like, "If you have an itch, what difference does it make which hand you use to scratch it?"

Clint thought of an itinerary for tomorrow and went to bed.

Over an omelette and coffee in the morning, Clint decided to go to Solarte and Bastimentos to check on storm damage. He was close to the Indios there, so could collect a little information the police couldn't. He would wait until the last wave of the storm front passed. Probably early tomorrow. The wave would hit Bocas about four o'clock. He could handle McDonald this morning. Quiroz and Larienze tomorrow. He may not have to worry, tomorrow.

He took his boat out and ran it for awhile to get it hot enough to evaporate all the water that had managed to get under the cowl, then headed to Solarte. He met several of his Indio friends and chatted. They were always up and working by seven. It was ten 'til when he got there. Magali insisted he have some hojaldras, coffee and patacones, so he sat with her and her husband, Milcare, and their two kids. Milcare said there wasn't much to say about McDonald, except he was a black foreigner with an attitude that would guarantee privacy – whether he wanted it or not.

"If everything's so horrible here in Panamá, why doesn't he return to Nassau?" Li asked. "Is there a reason he can't? Like they don't like his attitude there, either?"

There wasn't much more. Clint said he was checking to be sure everyone was alright and that there wasn't damage that couldn't be repaired before the next wave hit, in the afternoon. The natives had weathered storms a hell of a lot worse than this minor atmospheric disturbance. Clint said he knew it. He just wanted to be sure his friends were OK.

He stopped at two other places before coming in close to the McDonald finca. McDonald was on his dock, trying to get his boat up. It was sunk. McDonald was a bullish bald man with a lot of gold teeth. He was just fat enough to make him ugly as homemade sin, to Clint.

"Leave it there until tomorrow," Clint called. "There's another one coming in this afternoon, then it will clear up."

"I have to get the motherfucking motor off and try to dry it out, if it's any of your goddamned business!"

"Well, I could offer to help you. I could take my boat alongside and lift one side to dump some of the water, then it would float to where you could get the motor off – if there was a chance in hell you could handle a three hundred pound engine by yourself."

"Let's do that."

"Or I could treat you the way you've already treated me and decide to do one of two things," Clint continued. "I could tell you to fuck off and enjoy watching your shit ruin in the salt water, or I could say I'd help – for a hundred bucks."

McDonald grinned. "You, I could like. You aren't wimpy like these shitheads, here."

"They aren't wimpy. They simply treat people with respect until they get to know them well enough to know if they want anything to do with them. They've solidly decided they don't want anything to do with you. Push it, and you'll end up learning how wimpy they are, right quick!"

"I could take any three of them without working up a sweat!" he snarled.

"Maybe, before you turned into a fat out-of-shape pig, you could've taken one of them. They're small people. Right now, I'd say there isn't one of them who couldn't take you down, pretty fast."

He laughed. "OK. A hundred bucks. I got money up the ass."

"So do I," Clint replied. He went alongside the

sunken 18 footer and dropped the grapple anchor under the front, caught the molded seat underneath, and lifted. It slowly began to rise, then sluggishly dumped water over the motor in the rear. After about three minutes, about a third of the boat front was above the water. Clint let go and stepped hard on the front. The water leveled until the gunnel had about four inches above the water. He dropped his bail line into it and threw a five gallon bucket to McDonald and took one himself to throw water out. In a few minutes, it would remain afloat without any further hand bailing. Clint let the high-flow bailer from his boat draw a lot more of the water out. McDonald invited him to have some coffee or booze or whatever, so they left it running and went to the somewhat overdone stilt house, where Benson McDonald introduced his ladyfriend, Shirley LeGrande. They talked awhile. Clint brought up the drug boat and murder.

"I'm here because of drugs coming in through Nassau," Benson said. "I got into trouble with a bunch at a casino there. I had a little restaurant and beer bar. They started trading the shit right there. I threw them out, then the place burned down. I caught two of them one night in a dark alley and almost killed them. Their buddies have been after me, ever since."

"Not the same group, I hope?"

"I wouldn't know. I doubt it."

Shirley seemed to be a lot more friendly. They chatted, then Clint left. Benson had a tripod to take the motor off and into his bodega (shed) to dry it out. Clint told him to meet the people halfway and they would gladly go the other half. They were *not* going three quarters of the way.

He said he didn't want friends. He wanted to be left alone. Clint told Shirley that they wouldn't hold him against her. If she wanted friends, she could have them. She nodded.

Well, McDonald was out, as a suspect.

Clint visited with another Indio family. He helped them put a couple of sheets of zinc on the roof that had been blown off. This time it, was anchored. Before, it had a couple of heavy rocks holding it in place. The Indios noted, years ago, that the zinc-plated panels would rust where the nails went through, very quickly. If the zinc wasn't scratched through or holed, it would last for twenty years or more – so they didn't drive nails through it. Clint said they had kilometers of polypropylene rope, so why not tie it down? They did that. They would have to replace the rope about every five years. The sunlight broke it down.

The wind was picking up and it was getting

darker than Clint liked. He turned on the weather channel on his boat and learned this last storm front had intensified and would be a lot worse than the first two. The bay was getting pretty rough before Clint got home. He was protected from the worst of it, where he was, but people on the Caribbean side would get hit hard, this time.

Sergio had called several times, but Clint's cell was on the boat while he was working. He hadn't heard it. He called to learn that another tortured body had been found. This one on Isla Popa.

"It would seem you were correct in assuming that body found between Solarte and Bastimentos was nothing to do with the drug runner," Sergio admitted, when Clint went to the station, in the morning. "It perhaps has to do with drugs, but who knows?

"Have you anything new to report?"

"Other than that McDonald is a total ass, but has nothing to do with it, no. I'm going calling on Larienze and Quiroz in a bit."

"That's nice. So. Who are Quiroz and Larienze? Those unpopular people on Bastimentos?"

"Yeah. I want to see what their stories are."

Sergio nodded. He told Clint what they knew about body #2. Except that he could be a man who was around every once in awhile they called Carlos, they didn't have anything. It was pretty exactly the same kind of torture body #1 showed. It didn't mean too much, in itself.

"It means someone wants information that they didn't get from the first one," Clint pointed out. Sergio agreed. They didn't know if whoever got the information from #2.

Clint went to the regular places for gossip, then took his boat to Bastimentos. Quiroz had the much easier place to get to, so he went there first. Quiroz was an arrogant snob. He first called that his dock was a private one, so get out. Clint called out that he could return with a police boat or he could talk to Quiroz now. His choice.

He said to come on in, but make it damned brief. He didn't have time to waste with anything to do with Bocas del Toro and its cheap tourist-trap atmosphere.

Clint said he doubted very much that Xavier Quiroz had time for much of anything to do with anyone else.

"I'll say what my close Indigeno friends said about the last person I talked to about this. If you don't like Bocas, go the hell back where you came from – or are you in the same situation? Where he COULDN'T go back there? He was even more unpopular, where he knew people, than he was here, where he made it a point not to know anyone."

"I resent your attitude!" Quiroz snapped.

"Oh? Am I supposed to care, or simply say I'm matching your own?"

"Say what you have to say, then get out! I'm much to busy to spend time chatting with riff-raff!"

"I see. A real legend in your own mind," Clint countered. "You want it short, so that's how you get it.

"What's your connection to the drug shipment deterred yesterday in the bay?"

Quiroz sputtered and stared a minute, yelled that he didn't have anything to do with it. He wasn't in any way ever even suspected of having anything to do with drugs. He deeply resented the implication.

"Better get used to it. You place yourself under suspicion with your attitude. Do you think we don't know you don't have anything to keep you so, as you claimed, busy you don't have time to waste on riff-raff like me?"

He looked like he would explode. He sputtered a bit more, then turned around and stormed toward the house, yelling for Clint to get off his property, and to stay off.

He was up to something, but it wasn't to do with drugs. Clint would damned well see that he was investigated, carefully. Clint suspected he was only a deluded idiot who was being used by someone else as a distraction.

Which made it interesting. A distraction from what?

That would have to wait.

Larienze tried to be polite, but couldn't pull it

off. He had a very grating personality. He was another self-absorbed type who tried to act like one of the boys, but was condescending in almost everything he said. He didn't have a clue to what other people were thinking. He wouldn't be involved. He pictured himself as some kind of genius. He wouldn't fall for any line from anyone in this backwater. He kept within his regular group of friends. He was sure he was way ahead of the game.

Clint looked around at his location and the house he had built. He grinned to himself. He had probably paid at least three times what it was worth when he was told about the super-great deal available by one of those "friends."

Trouble now was that Clint was out of suspects. He went out toward the end of the island, where it was pretty isolated, to talk with some of his friends there. They didn't know much about any of it. They might have seen the dead guy around somewhere, but how would they know? They didn't even know what he looked like. The police had asked them about it, but didn't have a picture, or even a good description. "Have you ever seen the dead guy we found?" and not even be able to say what he looked like, whether he was a black, Indio, gringo, or what? How old was he? 17 or 70?

Clint had to agree that would be pointless, but he knew Sergio's methods. That stuff would be covered, later. If he got anyone to say the wrong thing, he would know that one knew more than he was telling. It could save weeks of investigating to have someone make that one little slip.

The eight or nine year old kids saw things that would open other things up a bit. He did learn that a boat had come to sit in a little cove when the police boats went in. It stayed there until the watcher boat at the mouth of the bay went to search more back inside, then left. That led to the father saying he saw it, but didn't want to get involved. That could be dangerous to his family. Clint said he would never be mentioned, in any way.

It was a 22 foot white and green boat with a center console. It had a canopy that was taken down when it was in the cove. It was a blue plastic cover that would show. There were three people in the boat. All men. It went around the end of the island and headed more or less straight in. It didn't go toward Bocas. One of the men had a gun. It may have been an AK-47, but they didn't see it close and weren't really concerned, or they would have found out more. They didn't tell the police. That would be dangerous. Clint would never let it be known who told him anything. The police; they could trust Sergio, but, if Sergio knew, soon everyone would know, and they would know who Sergio talked to. Sergio had to file reports that others could read.

Clint gave all the kids cookies he kept in his boat for that reason, thanked all of them, then headed back to Bocas. This was a break. The drug runner wasn't picked up by anyone on either of the islands. They went straight toward the mainland, so could have been heading to Popa. The one who tortured and killed #1 was on that boat. That meant the boat was out there to kill #1 and got an opportunity to make something with the drug boat. Maybe the runner was body #2. He would have offered them something valuable for their taking him to shore, away from Bocas or observation.

Then he would be stupid not to have made whatever he promised unavailable before he was on the mainland and safe. He wasn't body #2. Unless.... No. Someone known as Carlos was body #2, not some drug runner who had probably never been there before. Definitely not to the mainland.

Clint headed in. The runner would have been taken to Tierra Oscura. It was the only way to get him near a road, with that storm making everyone be home. He would have been seen and noted if they went ashore anywhere else where their passenger could get to a road. Everyone was watching the bay. The tone of the light and the direction and power of the wind told them a lot more facts about an approaching storm than any weatherman on TV possibly could.

He took care of what he had waiting, e-mail and such at home, then fueled his boat from the tank he kept at his place and headed to Tierra Oscura.

No one knew who might have come in the night to Tierra Oscura. They were all inside, or working to secure things for the next wave to come through. A couple heard the boat come in and heard what seemed like a small argument, then whoever it was left by the road. He got a taxi that was there from taking Lydia home. Clint said that would help. He talked to Lydia. She said the man who took the taxi called to it from down the road. She did hear him ask how much to take him to a bank and bring him back.

That meant he was from Panamá. He had to get to a bank to use the ATM. That would be in Almirante – if it had ever been fixed. It had sat since Christmas with a brick thrown through it. He might have to go to Changuinola.

Clint asked if she heard the answer. She wasn't sure, but she thought it was more than sixty dollars. The man had yelled something about sixty dollars, like he didn't believe it, but he did take the taxi.

Changuinola and back, barring obstructions or something. Two hours. Double the regular rate. Because of the storm. Half the time, if he went by boat to Bocas. He didn't want to do that. That meant the carrier came back in about two hours to collect.

He was a Latin man, about 5'10", strong, had longish hair. That was all she noticed. He wore a lot of rings and gold chains. She remembered that. He left them with somebody at the dock before he got the taxi. Maybe he was wearing those camouflage pants and a dark shirt.

Clint had found, years ago, to ask the minimum, then let them remember the rest, without a lot of pressure. The pressure would make them forget. We all notice a lot more about things than we realize.

How to find the taxi?

Simple! Very few would be running, that time of night. Only one would have gone to Tierra Oscura, then to Changuinola, then back to Tierra Oscura. It would be a regular Almirante taxi.

He headed back to his boat and to Almirante. It took four hours to find the taxi used. The driver said the guy stayed quiet, both ways. He took him to the machines at the Banco National, then brought him back. He left him in Tierra Oscura and came back home. He couldn't add much, except the guy used two or three different cards. He had over a thousand dollars when he got back in the taxi. He paid sixty five dollars.

He was just about what Lydia described. He spoke very good Panamanian Spanish. He used a cell phone at the bank, but not in the taxi. He seemed upset about something on the way back to Tierra Oscura.

The driver hadn't seen anyone else around, when he took the guy back to Tierra Oscura. There was no boat at the dock. The guy did use his phone again, but that was after they got to the dock and he was outside of the taxi. The taxi didn't hang around. It was late. He was tired and had made a good day with that passenger.

Clint soon went back to his boat. He could ask a few questions, now.

Back out to Bocas.

"We identified the person on Popa who was killed. Carlos Menendez. He and a man called Eduord Rauz hung around together, sometimes, and seemed to have money at times and be broke other times. I think perhaps Rauz will prove to be the first body. We have reports that they hung around Santiago and David, more than here. There are reports concerning an Eduord David from Panamá and Las Tablas. He has connections in Colón that caused him to be watched."

Clint told him about finding the route their runner had taken. He described the boat, as best he could. Sergio said Quenten Robinson had come in early in the morning. He claimed that he had stayed in Renaciamento with friends, for the night, and had come home when it was calm enough and light enough.

"Friend have a name?"

"Roberto David. He's bad news. We've run across him before. Two-bit thug and sneak thief."

"If he was with Robinson last night, he's the torturer. Him or Robinson."

"I would tend to agree. If we can get him to admit that they were, indeed, together, we can get them both, with little or no problem. There will be no way to explain why they were the only ones in the area of both killings. The MO was the same on both.

"You are not going to tell me how you obtained the information, are you?"

"Part of it. I went out to Tierra Oscura on an anonymous tip that a boat, as described, called at the dock, twice. It has proven to be the Robinson boat. You have enough to tag them. I'll find someone who saw that boat in there before the runner, and that it was not seen leaving, but was seen at the appropriate time with three people in it, very close to Solarte. While the police were there, in fact."

"Protect your friends, Clint. That particular branch of the Robinsons are known to intimidate people, and worse."

"I'll do that. You know it."

"Are you out of it, now?"

Clint thought for a moment. "No. There was a reason for that torture – at least, in the mind of the killer."

Sergio nodded.

Clint left and headed for home. He would find answers in Panamá City or David or Las Tablas. He wasn't about to go to Colón.

He got a flight to David. He would check out places, closest first. He had the pictures of David and Robinson from the police files. He had seen both, at times, in Bocas, but hadn't met or spoken to them. Robinson was black and David was mestizo. Robinson was bullish and a bit fat. David was thinner and sported a few tatoos. Both tended to too much flashy jewelry. David wore gang earrings on the left ear. He had a small diamond in a pierce on the nose.

Clint went to the Top Place billiard halls in

David, first, then to the lesser known pool halls. He found that David hung around a little place near the feria. They didn't think much of him, one way or another, but it was the kind of place where a big part of the business was with the type. It was the kind of place where Clint always kept a close watch behind – as well as in front, the sides and above. An altercation started while he was there, over a pool game. One punk hit another over the head with a pool cue. The other patrons broke it up and told them to sit down and cool off. They didn't find it at all unusual for one person to smack another with a cue stick. The tough-looking women ignored the whole scene.

Clint used his little special digital camera to take pictures of everyone, without them knowing. He drank one beer and left.

He found another place out toward Pedrigal, where David went at times. He was with Robinson, most of the times he went there. Robinson came in a few times, by himself, to meet someone named Enrique Castille. Castille was known as a mafia hood. People were scared of him.

Everyone was suspicious why Clint wanted to know anything. He said it wasn't any of their business, but he didn't mind saying his sister and her best friend might have a little something to do with it. They were minors. In Panamá, it wasn't considered as odd that a fifty something man had sisters that were minors. They were your sisters if your father was fifteen when you were born and seventy five when your sisters were born. It wasn't ever questioned if your parents were married or you were the result of a one night encounter.

David and Robinson weren't known to mingle, much, though they sometimes met people from Colón and Panamá (When we say Panamá with an extra stress on the final á we mean Panamá City). The people they met ranged from as scruffy as they were to a couple who seemed to be rather wealthy and out of place in such places. One was some kind of big lawyer or something. Geraldo Demerbens or something. They called him Mr. D.

They might be out of place because of the wealth, but not because of the type, Clint thought.

He went to the Palacio Imperial for the night. A palace it ain't, as the saying goes. He went around David for another day, but didn't learn anything new. He went to the Park Vista that night, where he met the owner, Peter, and some friends from Bocas who were in David on business or to buy things because the prices were so much better and more variety is available in David.

Next day was a short trip to Las Tablas. Neither

was welcomed there. It was rare for them to come.

Panamá City. Clint learned that they hung around a couple of places down past the end of Via España, from the police reports. They also were seen a lot in certain suburbs. Robinson sometimes met someone in a high-end restaurant and whorehouse, out a few kilometers.

Clint got an idea from that. He called a Russian semi-friend who was often in the place. He said he'd noted Robinson. He always met Juan Marinni, a Colombian who worked for some rather unsavory syndicates in Cali and Medillin. There was a connection with some wannabe gangster in Chiriqui, somewhere. Not so much drugs – though that tended to be a part of anything from Colombia – as kidnapping and such. "Protection" rackets were a large part of it. It was called "Private Insurance" there. It was the old mob thing from the states. They ran casinos and whorehouses. That kind of thing.

Clint had another name to work with. Maybe a connection with something. He'd heard of something that could finally connect something. A little something that connected Isla Popa and other places. It could explain why Carlos was tortured. It was a matter of finding how a scheme went wrong from the wrong end. It could tie all these people together – and Clint had been right when he said the drug runner had nothing to do with it, at all. All that happened, where he was concerned, was that he exposed Robinson and David, by accident.

Clint headed back to Bocas on the bus. He stopped for the night in Chiriqui Grande, but little was known, there. There were the usual stories about who was trying to steal whose land and how they were going about it. One story caught his attention, a little. It would fit what he suspected, but was the wrong person and wrong location. Almirante wasn't much different.

He got back to his place late enough that he went to dinner with Judi and Ben, where he was caught up on the latest gossip. Not much new. Both of them knew what to try to learn, if they didn't know why. He would go to Popa, in the morning. The answers were there – if he could find the right questions.

It was a little rough on the bays, but Clint got to Isla Popa around eight o'clock. Most of the men were at work, that late. Many of the women were at home. Clint stopped to talk with Dona and Yajaira and have a cup of coffee. They didn't know much about any of the things happening off the island. They knew of things that had happened on the island only from what they saw and heard. They did know that a body was found up toward the southeastern tip. There was some problem about that whole mess, because of the way those people from Colón were trying to force people off their land, there. The Martín family had started a big row about it, but had suddenly become silent. Paulo used to come to the little store/bar at least twice a week, with his wife and young daughter, but hadn't come in at all for more than two weeks.

Those people trying to buy the land for a fourth of what it was worth were nothing but gangsters and cheap thugs. The body found was working with someone that had something to do with that. So were two or three others.

Clint thanked them and headed for his boat. It

was a little rough on the tip, but he went around and found the dock to Martín's place in a little indentation in the shoreline. He went in to see a bright shiny new sign that said to keep out. Privado. He went in and tied to the dock. A man Clint had seen a few times around Bocas and Almirante came from the house with a big obvious thug type. Clint waved. The thug said, "Hey, gringo stupido! Can't you read?"

"Yeah, fuckhead. What do you want me to read to you?

"Hi, Paulo. Haven't seen you around for a few days. I was wondering if the storm did any damage, here. Some places were hit pretty hard by the winds."

The thug grabbed at Clint, who spun and came up under his chin to knock him into the water. He grabbed for the pistol in his belt when he came up, but Clint was over him with a pole that had been laying on the dock. He very calmly said to bring his hands up, empty, or he would suddenly be fish food.

The thug brought his hands into view and began swimming toward the shore at the dock base, when Clint waved him that way. Clint walked along above him with the pole at the ready. When the hood got to where he could stand, he moved on in with his hands held at head level. Clint reached out and took the revolver from his belt, when he was in kneedeep water. He told him to come on out onto the shore. He turned around on the bank and swung at Clint, throwing his other arm up to ward off the pole – which Clint had already dropped as he slipped to the side. The thug expected him to come up like before, and was ready for an attack from that direction.

Clint didn't come up like before. He came in from the side to where the thug had to twist toward him just in time to have a jarring right hook knock him to his knees. Martín cried for Clint to stop! He was making everything worse!

Clint saw the fear in Martín's eyes. He put a couple of things together, right then, and knocked the thug over his ear with the pistol butt. The thug dropped and was sprawled on the ground.

"Tell me about it," Clint demanded. "What's it about?"

"I don't know!" he wailed. "They want this land, for some reason. I won't sell, so they took my wife and daughter somewhere. They say they will kill them if I don't sell! They will pay me less than half of what it's worth, if I did want to sell it. If I get money they have all the legal papers and things to say it is theirs because they paid the money!"

"The one who was killed here night before last

was one of them?"

"Killed? I don't know about anyone being killed. The police came yesterday morning and asked Paco some questions, but he made me stay in the house. I don't know what it was about. He said it was just checking about the storm, but it wouldn't be that, because they never come out this far for that kind of thing."

"Was this shithead here night before last?"

"No. He tied me up in the afternoon and left. He didn't come back until early sunrise, yesterday morning. The police came about an hour later."

"If they know about this they will kill my wife and daughter. We have to do something!"

"I think I've heard a couple of things that will make it a bit easier to get them back. Let's get this punk conscious again," Clint said, as he took a small pail and filled it with water from the bay. He threw it in the thug's face.

Paco, as Martín had named him, came to, sat up, then suddenly lunged hard for Clint's legs with a long switchblade in his right hand. Clint stepped aside and brought a booted foot down hard on the hand with the knife in it. The thug squealed.

Clint said, in a very calm, but icy, voice, "I'm going to ask you a few questions that you will answer and maybe live, or refuse to answer and die. I'll use the methods on you that you used on

Carlos, capich?"

Paco grunted. He was holding his broken hand tight against his stomach with the other hand.

"Capich?" Clint said, even colder.

"They'll kill me if I say anything!"

"And I will if you don't. Hell of a position to be in, isn't it?

"What's this crap about?"

He looked like he would cry. His eyes darted around, but his position was hopeless, and he knew it. Clint might actually torture him to death, for all he knew. It was something he had done a few times.

"I don't know. Some kind of map or code or something."

Clint thought. There were some maps from when they discovered a pirate's chest full of gold and jewels. It was on a case where they were looking for a chest of money. Millions. They found two, one of which was a pirate's chest that some drug cartel people from Colombia had put a few million dollars in cash in fifty years ago. Those maps were checked and accounted for, to the least detail. Someone was running a scam against a mob boss with phony maps? Was anyone that stupid?

Clint asked what Carlos had done to make him get the treatment Rauz got. That missed in a surprising way.

"I don't know who Rauz is supposed to be. The police told me about Carlos Mendez."

"Rauz is the one you tortured and killed by Solarte."

Paco looked like a trapped animal. "No. That was Santamaria. Rosendo Santamaria. He tried to steal something from some people in David. We sent a message with the way he was handled. You can't let that start, or every two-bit creep in town will be stealing from you.

"Okay. You know about that, so you know I did the same thing to this Carlos character. Him, I caught sneaking around here when I came back. I found out he was working for somebody else who was interested in the maps and were trying to find a way to cut themselves in before he became incapable of saying anything."

"You mean someone is so stupid they'd try a stupid scam on *two* gangster bosses?" Clint said, unbelieving. "I thought it was phenomenally stupid to try to con one!"

"Scam?" The hood was very interested, all of a sudden.

"I want to talk to your boss. Now, but first get Martín's family back here. This is a stupid way to handle this kind of thing. I'll make a deal where your boss gets to do all the treasure hunting he wants, but he's *not* to involve innocent people, or I'll call my Russian friends in Panamá and your boss and everyone associated with him will become statistics in a couple of hours, at most. You only think you know how to cause pain. It was how some of the Ruskies made their living for years before they came here."

Almost anyone in organized (or, as seemed too apparent, in this case, disorganized) crime in Panamá is terrified of the Russian mob. They have the reputation of being totally merciless and more than a little crazy.

"Get the family released. Now!"

"I can't get them to do anything! I just take orders! I ain't no boss! Fuck!"

"Just tell them that Clint Faraday says he'll get his Russian friends to act, if they don't cooperate. They'll know I'm not the type to bluff. I have a small bit of a reputation, myself."

"I can call them and try. It wasn't my idea to grab the woman and kid. I told them that was stupid. It would only get too many others after their asses. You keep this stuff in the family. Somebody else, you don't know what's going to happen! *This* kind of stuff can happen!

"I ain't got a cel."

Clint handed him his cell, then had to punch the number and put the phone on speaker. Paco couldn't hold onto the phone and punch the number with one hand broken. He got someone he called "Juan" and argued a minute. He said to put the boss on the phone. It was an emergency. Juan refused.

"Mira, estupido! Diga Ger ... el es urgencia muy muy mal!"

Clint caught that and quickly added two and two. He remembered what he heard in David. "Tell him we know who all of you are. We don't bluff! Maybe Geraldo, better known as Mr. D, has more sense than you, Juan Marinni! Clear enough?"

There was a silence, then another voice came on. Paco gave him the message, then passed the phone to Clint.

"What is this about a scam?"

"First, the Martín family gets sent back home and are unharmed, in any way."

There was a short silence. "That was a very large mistake. I will grant that Paco was correct, in that. They arc not harmcd, and will be returned, immediately, if you will but guarantee that no action will be taken for our detaining them."

"IF they are unharmed, you have my guarantee – where they are concerned."

"You say I may seek the treasure you claim is not there without the application of pressure?"

"That was the stupidest part of this. I know it's

the way your group handles things, but it's time you move into the real world. You may use any of the methods the police and I used to find the treasure. You will simply give Mr. Martín or anyone else whose land the stuff's found on ten percent of the net. Nobody gets hurt, there's not a bunch of silly plots and plans, and your kids won't be ashamed of what their Pop was. Maybe you'll live and stay out of the pen long enough to have kids, if you don't already. I didn't check on that. We never involve others in our methods."

"He will agree to that?" Paulo looked surprised, shrugged and nodded.

"Certainly! You wouldn't if it was on your land and you wouldn't have to do a single thing, yourself, to find it?"

"Probably not. I'm not the sharing type. I see your point, however, and will agree.

"What is this about a scam?"

"If your map is from that deal where we dug up those two chests, every map Miss Halverson had was checked, thoroughly. One of the chests was there. The other two had been found as much as ninety years ago. There weren't any maps secretly hidden or any other cache of maps found. The other pirate wasn't nearly successful enough to have much hidden. The Cano cruds would handle anyone who got any map to what they consider as their property. Despite it all, there's still a lot of power with some people in that. There are no Canos alive who were involved. There are several people alive who are not Canos – or not known to be Canos. Don't forget how many people here have two families that don't know diddly about each other."

"So I have heard. Very well. May I again speak with Paco?"

Clint passed the phone back. Paco talked a moment. He told Geraldo about Carlos. He then passed the phone back to Clint.

"Mr. Faraday, do you know who this Carlos person was working with?"

"No. I also have to find Rauz. Paco says he wasn't the one who he hit over by Solarte. That leaves some interesting possibilities open. That leaves some questions I'll get answers to."

"If you will be so kind as to inform me, should you learn that name?"

Clint thought about it. "I'll give a conditional yes to that. No one else not directly involved will be bothered."

"Thank you. The people will be back home within the hour. Paco will leave the area. I'm certain that you will describe his part in this to your police associates. As a favor, please wait until you can report that the family is home safely and see that Paco has means and opportunity to escape the area.."

"For this, they can pick him up anywhere they find him."

"Only in Panamá. I will assure you that he will not too long remain in Panamá."

Clint agreed. It would be better for these type to handle it, themselves. So long as they only killed and tortured others of the same type, in the same business, it was saving the police time and money.

Clint waited at the dock, after taking Paco there, until a taxi brought the Martíns to Tierra Oscura. He took them home and headed back to Bocas.

He really did want to know what happened to Rauz. Was he tied up in it? Carlos was. It was likely. What was the connection with Rosendo Santamaria? Who was Rosendo Santamaria?

Who was trying to run a scam on those kinds of people? Were they crazy, stupid – or both? If Paco was the one on the boat with Robinson, what is David's connection to this, if any?

There was Geraldo. David figured in it, somewhere. He was seen talking with ... so that's part of it. He was checking to see what Geraldo knew and what he was doing.

Was whoever he was working for running the scam?

Finding out would be a good way to pass the

time. He would have to go back to David, in the morning. Rauz would be there, or in Panamá City. Clint could find him.

He got in to his dock, cleaned up the boat, refueled it, called Judi, and cleaned up. He would spend tonight doing little or nothing. He and Judi would try the 9 Degrees. Rick was a gourmand. The food would be exceptional, if expensive.

It was a very good night. Clint caught Judi up to date on things. She would always be invaluable in finding certain kinds of information. She would hold down the Bocas end and he would spend a few days in the David area.

In the morning, he got the early water taxi to Almirante and headed on to David. He met a friend, Santo Guerra, from Tierra Oscura, when he boarded the bus at the 46KM marker. They talked most of the way to Chiriqui Grande.

Clint decided to spend the day in Punta Peña. Santo said there was some kind of problem in that area, or in Mali. It sounded too much like someone was looking for a spot on a map, in that area. That was too far inland for any pirate chest. What was going on, now?

Elena, the waitress at the little restaurante past the school, had heard some people talking who were looking for something. They had a map on the table and had asked her if she knew where there was a big rock shaped like a turtle on the side of a mountain near the river. She had told them she didn't know of any such rock. She hadn't paid much attention to the map. It was a computer copy or something. It wasn't like a plano. It was mostly lines with notations in some foreign language.

Interesting. That river wasn't navigable. It never had been. Whenever the water was deep enough to go in with a small cayuga, the water was too swift that far up and was too filled with rapids. There were a lot of smaller stretches that could be used, but the usable connection with the Caribbean wasn't there. This wasn't connected.

Was it?

Elena and Virginia described the three men. One large and fat black man and two who could have been Panamanians with gringo or European parents on one side. They only called the black

Gordo, but one of the others was Tomás Something. The other was called Ricky. They all spoke Spanish without accent from any other place. They didn't use any Colombian or Costa Rican words or expressions.

That would mean Ricky was named Enrique – unless he had a parent from an English-speaking country. It could be Richard or Ricardo. No one had seen any of them around, before, except the one called Ricky, who had come two weeks before, looking for someone called Ed.

Eduord Rauz?

All they knew was Ed.

If it was Eduord Rauz, this was most likely connected. If not ... it could be or not.

Clint caught the next bus for David. He got there a little after four and checked into the Pensión Costa Rica. He went to Peter's bar (everyone called the Park Vista Peter's) at the Hotel Iris, where he talked with several people about whatever came up. He didn't learn anything. He went to the pensión and sacked out for the night. In the morning, Clint headed for Pedrigal. He may find an answer or two there.

He didn't. He went back to David and to the pool hall David hung around. He mostly listened. He caught a snatch of conversation about Geraldo having a mad on about something or someone.

Nothing that he could connect.

That was the problem, here. Nothing to connect anything to anything else.

A rather obvious puta came to ask him if he was looking for sex. He said, "Yes. With just about anyone but you."

She didn't know how to take that, so went back to sit at a stool at the end of the bar. An hour later, he left. There would be some kind of party that night they were talking about that most of them were invited to. Clint figured it might be a good idea to crash it. In disguise. It seemed Mr. D was paying for the food and beer, but other drinks were not included.

Clint went back to sit for a beer in a couple of other places. He heard one bit in The Top Place Billares about someone called Rosendo, who had disappeared.

That reminded Clint. He called Sergio and asked what had been learned.

Rosendo Santamaria was identified by a supposed girlfriend, who said he was supposed to come to her place, but had never arrived. She wasn't from the Bocas area – so why would she be looking for someone else to arrive at a place she had rented yesterday morning?

She would be watched very closely, but also discreetly. Sergio also wanted to know who else she knew or met with, there.

David had gone through Sixola into Costa Rica, also yesterday morning. Another little clue that didn't quite connect. Was he running from someone?

Likely. Who? The woman who identified Rosendo?

Not enough information.

Clint decided he was off on some kind of wild tangent. Maybe something would come together at the party.

He went back to the pensión to clean up and put on a disguise. The man who left the Costa Rica about seven thirty was a bit seedy and tough-looking. He had very black hair that didn't quite match his complexion and wore cheap cologne. He had a couple of rings that were semi-precious stones and an earring that was a very good diamond. He had on some heavy gold-plated chains. He had a scar on the side of his face that was covered with makcup, but not quite. His moustache didn't quite manage to match the color of his hair and wasn't well-kept.

He got to the pool hall, but was stopped at the door. There was a private party inside.

"Yeah, yeah. Mr. D said to drop by."

"Mr. D?"

"Ger. What?" Clint snarled.

He was passed through, after saying his name was Culebra (Snake) Smith. There were about thirty people inside. A truly mixed bag of seedy thugs and men in good business suits. (Probably lawyers. Very few but bankers and lawyers wore suits in Panamá: You know how to tell a lawyer? You can't, but you can always tell *who's* a lawyer because he's wearing a suit.)(It doesn't translate very well.) Puta's and ladies in good clothes.

Clint watched the doorman go to a heavy man with somewhat long, wavy hair. He was smoking a Cuban cigar and had on a massive gold ring. The bouncer pointed to Clint. The man shrugged and came over.

"Mr. D?" Clint asked, before he could say anything. "I'm afraid I used your name to get in."

The voice from the telephone call in Bocas replied, "Mr. Faraday? You are nothing like was described to me. I was waiting for you."

"Waiting? For me?"

"Yes. I am aware of some of your methods, so arranged this get-together to introduce you to a number of people. One of those here is the person we seek, I am quite sure."

"No. That person will have several people here to observe. It's very slightly out of character for you to throw a party on such short notice. They'll be suspicious. They'll definitely watch who you talk to. It might be a good idea to have me unobtrusively removed. You stay awhile and begin checking your watch in a half hour or so, get a tiny bit upset, and leave, after another half hour. They'll believe you were waiting for someone who won't show up. Then they'll figure I decided not to work with you and figured the angle of this party. It'll keep my cover and tell them some things. Not knowing you, directly, could be to our advantage. They won't recognize me in this getup. Clint is, so far as they can learn, in his room for the night, too tired to go out.

"They'll have me followed. I'll go to the place Clint Faraday is staying. Maybe they'll decide I'm some hood working for me."

He started to smile, caught himself, got a bit of a wary look, turned, and walked off. He spoke to the bouncer a moment, then the bouncer came to tell Clint, as Mr. D said, he wasn't welcome there. It would be better, all around, if Clint were to decide to go elsewhere. Clint looked over to Geraldo and mouthed, "Asshole!" and handed the bouncer his half-finished beer. He stalked out. Geraldo gave the bouncer a high thumbs up and started a conversation with an attractive woman as Clint passed out the door.

Clint noted the one who followed him. He took one of the taxi's waiting out front and the woman took another, almost immediately. That driver didn't know how to follow anyone without being obvious to an almost comical degree. Clint decided to have a little fun, so spent until well after midnight, going from dive to dive. She had to be in or out front of them to keep him in sight, which made her even more obvious. There's almost no one on the streets in David after ten o'clock, but she couldn't very well show up in every place he went to. A woman standing in front of a cheap bar at eleven o'clock and later was assumed by everyone who saw her to be a hooker. Clint would bet she had an interesting, if not too pleasant, night. Particularly after it started raining at ten twenty.

There were no taxis in the area he managed to be when he decided to go back to the pensión. She was following about a block back. Clint was wearing a thin waterproof sweater, as was the custom at night in the rainy season. She was wearing a thin evening dress. After about six blocks, Clint managed to flag a passing taxi. She was standing on the corner a block back and began desperately trying to flag a taxi, herself. She must have found one, because a taxi pulled up close behind and followed them to the Costa Rica. Clint got out and paid his taxi. Her taxi was pulled into the lot at the bakery across the street. Two cars on the entire street, both taxis, one in front of the pensión, one across the street at a bakery. Clint had the giggles as he rang to be let in. He spoke to the desk girl, quickly, then waited just inside the steel doors until the signal rang and the desk girl keyed for it to open. The woman was standing there, but couldn't come inside. There were no available rooms, and she wasn't a guest, so wouldn't be allowed past the doors.

She asked about Clint, who was just on the side where he couldn't be seen from the door. The girl said Clint was in his room. He hadn't left since she came on duty. He was obviously exhausted and said he was not to be disturbed. He would not be disturbed.

She asked about the man who just came in.

If she didn't know the name of the man who just came in, she had no business there.

Now she could find a place to watch the front of the place for the rest of the night, or leave. She went over to in front of the Universidad Latina, talked to the night watchman for a couple of minutes, then walked toward downtown.

Clint went to his room, took off the disguise, took a shower, and went to bed.

The morning was clear, and a bit cool. Clint went to Doña Amelia's for breakfast. He was the first customer. He had been walking around for more than half an hour. He woke up before David got into motion, much. He liked to walk around the city while it was quiet.

After the good breakfast (hojaldras and coffee with an omelette) he strolled past the Alcalá. He had seen a man at the party, there, the day before. Clint had a talent to note people and places, automatically. He could place them when he saw them again. When the restaurant opened, he went in to have coffee, then acted like he was waiting for someone for ten or fifteen minutes, went to the desk to ask if Mr. Alexander was still in his room. The woman checked the register and said they had no one by that name registered.

Clint also read upside down, as well as right side up. He noted all the names and times in the register, shook his head, and said they would have come in about eight the night before. The Alcalá was full by six thirty. They may have gone elsewhere.

Clint thanked her and said they were the type to go to the Best Western, then. He'd probably missed them. He went to the café across the street for a chicha (fruit drink) and more coffee. The man and a woman came out and went toward centro. Clint casually finished his chicha and left when they were a block and a half away. He followed them to the Multi-Café by the Hotel Castilla, where they came out on the porch to sit with another man and woman. This one was also in a suit. They had some papers the second one took out of a briefcase and were discussing when Clint walked by, four feet away. He'd seen Freddy, a local character, sitting on the wall in front and went to sit with him and say good day. The wall was three feet from the table. Tom and Gene, two other gringos who were there most mornings, came out to greet him as they sat at their regular table, five minutes later. The lawyers were lawyers and were discussing a case. One was defending and one was prosecuting. They were making a crooked deal, where they both made a bundle and the people they supposedly represented would get it in the ass from both. Very typical.

Freddy told Clint they came about once a week to figure ways to screw everybody in sight. He knew them. He would report to their clients what was going on. They could believe him and do something, or get screwed. Their choice.

Clint grinned and agreed. Another dead end. Clint went back to the Costa Rica to think.

Who would have a clue? Geraldo was one side of it. That part was solved. Now he was angling for Clint to show him who he was up against. He probably had some ideas, but wouldn't give. This was someone who was either nuts or very dangerously crafty.

Clint spent some time thinking. He put everything else out of his mind and went over only what had to do with this. He decided someone was trying to pit Geraldo against another smalltime crime boss. He would have to discover why, to learn who – unless there was a way to force the issue.

He grinned. There just might be!

The next stop was the marina, at Pedrigal. Clint did note one person at that party who worked there. He had a large boat and was some kind of partner, or something. He had a good reputation, but was known to be into a few slightly shady deals. Nothing that was likely to hurt anyone who couldn't afford it. He had a philosophy that said certain things were games. The loser had to pay. Don't bother to get into the game with anyone who couldn't be depended upon to have the funds to pay. Damned sure, you don't get into it if *you* don't have the funds!

He was on the dock, giving instructions to the workers about pulling a large yacht and painting the hull. There were some minor repairs while it was out of the water.

"Hi, Harry. Nice job!" Clint greeted, pointing at

the boat.

"Triple-overpriced, thus very expensive to keep up. Holloway can afford it, and ten more like it. His IQ is about his shoe size.

"What's up?"

"Damned little, except taxes, rainfall, and my deficit," Clint replied. That was a joke between them.

"Found anymore pirate treasure?"

"Not looking for any. Wasn't looking for that."

"Yeah. You don't give a damn, so you find three damned treasure chests. I care a bunch, and can't find more than a centavo laying in the street."

Clint raised an eyebrow and cocked his head to the side, looking at the boat. Harry laughed. He said he didn't find that. It found him. "Any luck with this latest map thing?"

"Which latest map thing? I was looking for some guy who killed some other guy, found him and decided it would be much better for everyone concerned if he just left Panamá. The cops here don't need all their time taken trying to prosecute mobsters who'll get away with it, in the long run, anyhow.

"What about a map? I thought they found all of that crap."

Harry looked a bit startled. He said, "Uh, I heard there was some kind of map to a lost gold mine out there, uh, somewhere. Maybe Rambala or that area."

"Oh. I heard something about that in Punta Peña. They have to find a certain rock near a mountain on a river or something as stupid. Any rock like that would have been down the river a century ago. Hell, look at the size of those rocks the innundation took down the river! One of them up near Fortuna was bigger than that boat! I watched it, perched on the edge, for three weeks, then it was gone. A couple of hundred meters, straight down. Who the hell would look for a gold mine over there? It's not that kind of place. Gold isn't found in sandstone and calcium types of rock. It's found in silica-based formations."

"Pretty much what I figured. I suppose they think some old Indio will remember it and where it was. Or something. You never know where there's a little lode."

A man came from the office to tell Harry that Gordo said he would be there in an hour.

Gordo was a common name. It meant nothing, until Harry seemed to know a hell of a lot about somebody looking for a gold mine near Punta Peña. Clint chatted for a few minutes, then waved and left. He would be where he could get a look at Gordo, when he arrived. He might have finally found a bit of a connection – but what did it connect?

When Gordo showed up, it was clear this was one of the people in Punta Peña. Nobody else could be that close a description.

What was a person like Harry into that would get him tied up with a bunch of small-time gangsters? Clint could see where they might try to move in on his marina. It was a place that could be used in any number of ways to garner the odd crooked dollar or thousand. He would be in the position where they would try to move in on him, though. It could mean very big problems, a little ways down the line. Harry was far too smart to fall for a gold mine scam. What was going on?

Clint got a truly evil leer on his face. Harry was too smart to fall for that kind of scam. They were the type who would definitely try to move in on his business. They would believe anybody who came to them for "financing" a search for a lost gold mine that the someone had a map about.

He was smart enough to set up the scam! He heard about the maps from the pirate treasure deal and decided he could get the two hoods pitted against one another, then could sit aside and watch the fun.

Okay. For the tale, Harry had a couple of opposing gangsters who were trying to take over his marina operation. He was smart enough to pit them against each other. His name wouldn't show up. Ever. He made the slip to Clint, who he trusted. He wouldn't slip like that, where those types were concerned.

Clint wanted the whole story. He would get it. It might be fun to get those types fighting. The only thing was that Clint would see to it nobody else, like the Martín family, were brought into it. That took the fun out of it. Harry hadn't even considered that. He wouldn't start anything that he thought would involve innocent people.

When Gordo left, Clint strolled back into the office. Harry looked a bit wary. He tried to tell Clint something with his eyes and expression and a very slight shake of his head. He pulled at the lobe of an ear.

There was some kind of listening device in place.

"Just wanted to ask if you know of a rig like that one you're pulling for sale. Not as big, and a good deal. I'm not somebody with money for ten boats. Something cheap to maintain."

"There's no such thing as a large boat that's cheap to maintain," Harry replied, with a grin. Clint had let him know he caught the hints about the listener.

"Here. Call me if you find anything. I'll be in David tonight, but back in Bocas tomorrow or the next day, if things go as planned. It's my cel, so it gets me anywhere." He handed Harry a slip with his cell number on it. There was a name on the slip on the other side. Hanrady.

Harry nodded. "I might go to David tonight. I need a good meal of something other than fish. That's better here than anywhere else, but not ten nights in a row."

"Try Las Brasas," Clint suggested. "Best rib-eye in the area."

"Know something? I think I haven't had a good steak in the last five years. I'll have to try the place one day. Tonight will probably be that new Itallian place near where Panamá Bill's used to be."

Clint waved and went out. He headed back to David. Harry would be at La Tipica tonight. He would expect someone to be watching the Itallian restaurant and Las Brasas. La Tipica had great mariscos (seafood) that Harry said he was tired of. Clint loved their camarones apanada (breaded shrimp). Harry did most of his own cooking, so wouldn't have to eat seafood ten nights in a row. He knew Clint well enough to know he got what the message was. Clint would be at La Tipica in a disguise that Harry knew. Destin Hanrady. A cousin who only existed at odd times. An easy disguise, because he looked a lot like Clint.

Never attack at center. Come from a close angle, at times. Nobody will detect it. The purloined letter, with a different stamp on the envelope. Clint had found it effective. "Destin" sported a neat moustache and was a little shorter and not in as good a condition. He was ten years younger than Clint, but looked almost like he could be a brother. Clint did most of it with clothes and some very good makeup. The effect was what he wanted, when he left the pensión through the restaurant under construction on the side. Very few people knew how to go directly from the pensión into the patio and through.

He was in La Tipica about twenty minutes when Gordo and Harry came in. Harry waved and said he saw him at the marina, earlier. He hadn't found anything yet, but he was looking. They went to a side table and ordered a pitcher of beer.

Clint waited. They left about three quarters of an hour later. As they walked by, Harry did a hand down flat. He wanted Clint to wait there. He came back in about fifteen minutes, stayed in his car, and waved for Clint to come. Clint stood, stretched and went out to the lot. He waited behind Harry's SUV, so Harry knew he suspected he was being followed. A taxi came between the restaurant and Harry's SUV to let some people out. When it pulled away Clint was gone. Harry pulled out as a man who Clint had seen around earlier ran out to flag a passing taxi. Clint was out of sight from him, low in the seat.

Harry drove on to Las Brasas. The followers would definitely not look for him there, now. They thought he had headed back to Pedrigal. He parked behind and he and Clint went in.

Clint and Harry talked for the hour and a half they took to enjoy the excellent food. He was pretty much on track with what he suspected. Harry was a bit worried, because of the Martín family. He never thought anyone would be that stupid. Clint said that was the way great grandpa did it, so it's the way I do it. Geraldo, at least, wouldn't do that kind of thing again. Clint had hinted that it was a scam.

"Oh, he expects it to be a scam. He just thinks someone else is working it. The someone else thinks he's working ... that's what has me worried. The gold mine was something Geraldo wasn't supposed to know about. Yet."

"Who is the someone else?" Clint asked.

"Ramos. He's the other two-bit who thinks he can crowd me into letting him buy a partnership in the marina."

"I'm not familiar with him."

"Same type. From the Panamá area. Runs women and some dope. Into protection. Murder for hire – cheap."

Clint nodded. He didn't doubt the type. He just

didn't know who. Now he did.

"Clint, it's going on too long and it's gone too far. How can we end it?

"I'm assuming you're with me, on this."

"For a bit of a, shall we say, partnership, I'll have my guys handle it for you."

That got Clint the bird. He laughed.

"Maybe we can ... I do have an in. I'd like to get that kind of cruds out of the equation. Be deaf, mute, blind and stupid about me and anything concerned you might hear. I assume Gordo is working for this Ramos character, but you're not supposed to suspect anything?"

Harry nodded. He grinned.

"They suspect a scam. Geraldo suspects a scam. They're both waiting for confirmation of a name. You give Ramos Geraldo and I'll give Geraldo Ramos. Just make damned sure the slimeball doesn't involve anyone else in his little vendetta that started in a couple of hours or three.

"Give Gordo the name as a sort of 'I wonder if he...' or 'I wonder why...' kind of slip of the tongue.

"I can assume the only things Gordo knows is because you sometimes say things before you think, where he can hear?"

"Now, why would I do that?"

This time, Harry got the bird.

Clint finished the meal and got a taxi, while Harry headed on out toward Pedrigal. When he got to the pension, he went in the way he'd come out, got rid of the disguise, and went to Peter's. He talked with several people there, at random, where the watcher could note them. He spoke with some tourists from Nicaragua for a few minutes. They would be going home early in the morning. Geraldo wouldn't have time to check them out, if that was what he was doing when Clint talked with anyone. He talked with a couple from Colombia, several Panameños, and some gringos. He went downstairs and stood just outside the stairway to call Geraldo. He said he didn't really have anything to report. All he heard was that someone named Ramos was into something that may or may not have anything to do with it – though a gold mine and treasure maps came up as part of what the guy was into or asking about or something. Did Geraldo find any type of possible connection with anyone with that name or something like it? There was a pause, then a few rather vulgar epithets, then Geraldo said he was one that he'd suspected was into it, but that he'd never thought would have the guts to try any such thing.

Clint went to the pensión and to bed. Tomorrow might be an interesting day.

"...just coming in. Several known malditos were involved in a shootout in Los Abanicos that ... one moment."

The screen changed into the noticias of a news event in progress. A scene with police cars and people hiding, as best they could, behind them was on the screen. There was a very nice house with a strong steel grate fence to one side. Shots were fired at the police cars from the house. The police answered with automatic weapons.

"The police report that the persons inside are known criminals who seem, at this time, to be involved in a gang war with others who broke down the gate just in the background of our picture by driving a large truck through it. Little is known, except that there are several bodies on the lawn. We cannot get close enough to see them here. No police have been injured. The bodies are those of members of both gangs, according to reports. We will stay here with our cameras and this reporter will report any and all things that transpire as they happen."

The windows and windshield of a police car near the reporter exploded when hit by automatic weapons fire. The reporter dove down behind the camera van. The picture was suddenly the tire of the van. It moved quickly up the side of the van and to the reporter, who was crouched down beside the driver's door, with the microphone clutched in her hand. She gasped that there were more shots fired that had come terrifyingly close. She was moving to a safer position. The scene shifted back to the studio.

Clint grinned and went to breakfast. The police knew how to handle this. None of the people around would be hurt, if they followed orders. Clint was sure not one person in that house would survive. The report would be that the police finally were able to enter and all of them inside had already killed each other. There would be no survivors.

The TV at the little local restaurant had the scene. The reporter from before was saying that the owner of the house, a Sr. Ramos, was long suspected of mobster connections, but there was never evidence to convict him of anything. There was a rumor that the rival gang was led by someone known only as Sr. D to the reporter. This seemed to be connected with an attack on Sr. D by members of the Ramos gang. Something had happened that brought the rivalry between the two gang lords to attacking each other at almost the same time. Investigation into the causes of the violence would have to wait until the violence was ended. It was believed that Sr. Ramos was in the house under attack in Los Abanicos, as Sr. D was in his house that was attacked at nearly the same time in Pedrigal. If the attack in Pedrigal was at all like this one, it was most unlikely either of them survived.

Clint called Harry, who said he didn't wake up this early. It was only six o'clock!

"Turn on TVN. Have a nice day," Clint replied.

"Already?"

"They were both ready. Neither thought the other was. We can now write those two and their goons into a footnote in the history of penny-ante wannabes. I'll head back to Bocas, I guess."

"Don't fall for any treasure maps or goldmine maps or any scams like that."

"Promise!"

Clint sighed, watched the TV for a few minutes, ate his chuleta and rice with sweetened fried bananas and beans, then had a salad of papaya, pineapple, apple, manzana de agua, melón and pear, with a mayonaise type of dressing and a guanabana chicha. Nowhere else in the world could you find a breakfast like that.

Clint again thought of how much he loved Panamá.

Clint looked out over the bay, and smiled. He raised his coffee cup to Judi, who was checking her plants on her deck. She called that she would come over. He could fix her a cup of coffee.

He went inside to check his computer. Nothing new.

Judi came in and said there were some rumors that a couple of gangsters were going to start a war over some old maps or something, and that the Martín family had been kidnapped, but were back home. Nothing else that caught anyone's attention. Wild Bill couldn't find a lawyer willing to take his already lost case. Some detective from the states was buying a big island down off of Chiriqui Grande. Some multibillionaire friend of Dave's who had a bellyful of the states.

Clint told her what had happened in David. She was a bit shocked he would set those hoods up, but she had to agree it was better than having them around and interfering with the police and abducting innocent bystanders.

Maybe Clint was getting pragmatic enough to see the best way out of a bad situation. Finally.

Nothing else was important enough to catch their attention, at the moment. They decided to go into the mountains to visit with some of their Indio friends. Maybe they could make a few more. Judi said Dave would go along.

"Oh, yes. Dave's live-in has decided to move to Las Tablas. She really likes it there, where shed has a couple of friends from the states who have been there three or four years."

"Selma? I guess Dave will be upset about that."

"No. That was always the deal. They're very comfortable with things as they're going. Dave says he's to old for commitments. Selma is as independent as he is. He'll visit at times, she'll come here at times, or to his place in David."

"Did he ever get that straightened out? I know he owns two houses there, but they ended up in some crook's name."

"He's still waiting for the police and courts to do something, other than make excuses and delay after delay. He'll get a few hundred of his Indio friends and take the places back. Even the local excuse for the mafia doesn't want a hundred Indios kicking their asses every time they step out the front door. That's more or less how you have to do anything."

"What the hell? He's getting pragmatic, too? A pragmatic cynic?"

"I guess. I'll call him. The detective moving to the island is a friend of Selma's. She says to wait until I get a look at his wife. She makes Playboy Bunnies look like drudges. If she wasn't such a great person and friend, she'd hate the bitch on general principles."

They chatted awhile as they collected what they'd take into the mountains. Besides a camera, Clint wouldn't take much. Dave came over to ask where they planned to go, so he'd know whether to take anything special. They said they hadn't gotten that far, so he suggested inland from the Tierra Oscura peninsula. He hadn't gone more than a kilometer or so into that area. It would be in the comarca, but they were all welcome there.

Clint threw a shirt, underwear, toothbrush and such in a small backpack. If they went to one of Dave's friend's places up there, they'd be there at least one night. They set out for the mainland in Clint's boat. It would probably not rain today, but who knew? Or cared?

C. D. Moulton's works are available on most major outlets as printed or e-books. CD writes the CD Grimes, PI, mysteries, the Det. Lt. Nick Storie mysteries, the Clint Faraday mysteries, the Flight of the Maita science fiction series, books on orchid culture and many others of many types. Mystery, adventure, intrigue, science fiction, humor, fantasy, paranormal, mild erotica, and factual.